I'm My Mommy

My mommy took me to the zoo. We saw
bears and monkeys, and they let us help feed
the seals.

I'M MY MOMMY

by Daniel Wilcox
illustrated by Mel Crawford

A SESAME STREET BOOK

Published by Western Publishing Company, Inc., in conjunction with Children's Television Workshop.

0-307-10499-0

Eighth Printing, 1978

I was thinking, and I thought up a good game to play.

"Let's pretend, Mommy," I said. "Let's pretend that I'm the mommy, and you can be the daughter."

My mommy thought about it.

"You mean," she said, "I'll pretend to be you, and I'll do all the things you do when we visit the zoo?"

I said, "Yes, and I'll pretend to be *you*, and *I'll* do all the things *you* do."

"All right, *Mommy*," said my mommy, and she laughed and began to skip.

She skipped right off. I had to run to keep up with her.

She skipped straight up to a balloon woman.

"Look, Mommy!" said my mommy. "Balloons! May I have one? Huh? Please? May I?"

"Why, certainly, Daughter," I said, and I told the woman to give my daughter a balloon.

First the woman looked at me funny, but then she handed my daughter a balloon.

I told my mommy, "You hold on tight to that balloon. Don't let it fly away."

I know she didn't *mean* to be careless, but she did let go.

"Mommy!" said my mommy. "My balloon flew away!" She began to cry.

I think she was afraid I'd be angry at her.

So I said, "Don't worry, Daughter. Accidents do happen. I'll buy you another balloon."

This time I made the balloon woman tie the balloon to my mommy's wrist, and then it couldn't fly away.

It made me happy to see how happy my daughter looked.

We walked along. Suddenly I heard the loudest, scariest sound I had ever heard.

It went, "ROARRRRRRRRRRRRRRRRRR!"

A big, ferocious lion was roaring at us!

"Mommy!" cried my mommy. "The lion roared at me! I'm frightened!"

"Me, too!" I said, and I hid.

Then I remembered. I was supposed to be my mommy. Mommies aren't afraid of lions . . . not when the lions are in cages.

So I said, "Daughter, don't be frightened. The lion is safe in his cage, and roaring is just his way of saying hello."

I waved at him and said, "Hello, Mr. Lion." He just looked at me, and then he didn't seem so scary anymore.

My daughter waved at him, too, and said, "Hello." I was proud of her.

As we walked off, my daughter said, "Mommy! I'm thirsty!"

"So am I," I said. "And look, Daughter—there's a water fountain."

We went over to the fountain. My mommy started to lift me up so I could drink. Then I remembered that I was my mommy.

So I said, "No, Daughter, you drink first. I'll lift you up."

"Are you sure, Mommy?" asked my mommy.

"I'm sure, Daughter," I said. "Mother knows best about these things."

I lifted her up.

When she finished drinking, I put her down.
Then my mommy looked at her watch and
said, "It's time to go home."

I said, "No! I wanna stay! I like the zoo!" But
then I remembered I was my mommy. So I said,
"Daughter, I'm afraid it's time to go home."

She said, "No! I wanna stay! I like the zoo!"
Kids are like that.

We went to the subway. It took me a while to buy a token because the window was so high. But nobody minded. My daughter didn't mind at all.

When we sat down, I said, "Mommy? Let's stop pretending now. I'll be the daughter again, and you be the mommy again."

"All right, Daughter," said my mommy, and she put her arm around me.

I was tired.

I was thinking. I never knew before how many things mommies have to do.

They have to keep balloons from flying away. They have to cheer up sad kids. They have to say hello to lions. They have to lift kids up to water fountains. They have to say when it's time to go. They have to buy subway tokens.

They have to do lots of other things, too.

"Mommy," I asked, "is it hard to be a mommy?"

"Sometimes," she said, "but I like it."
She gave me a hug.

If you want to read the other half of this book, close the book,
turn it over, and start again.

I was thinking. I never knew before how many things daddies have to do.

They have to touch worms. They have to kiss hurts. They have to help children out of trees. They have to say when it's time to go. They have to pay bus fares.

They have to do lots of other things, too.

"Daddy," I asked, "is it hard to be a daddy?"

"Sometimes," he said, "but I think it's fun, too.
I like it, Son."
He gave me a hug.

If you want to read the other half of this book, close the book,
turn it over, and start again.

But he climbed too high, of course.

"Daddy!" he shouted. "I don't know how to get down! I'm frightened!"

"I *told* you not to climb too high," I sighed. "Hold on, Son. I'll help you down."

I helped him down.

Then Daddy whispered to me, "It's time to go home."

"I don't wanna! I'm having fun!" I said.

Then I remembered I was my daddy.

So I said, "Son, I'm afraid it's time to go home."

"I don't wanna! I'm having fun!" he said.

Kids are like that.

On the bus going home, I paid the fare. The bus driver let my son ride for free, but I had to pay for myself.

When we sat down, I said, "Daddy? Let's stop pretending now. I'll be the son again, and you be the daddy again."

"All right, Son," he said, and he put his arm around me.

I was tired.

"Now how do you feel, Son?" I asked him.

"Much better, thank you, Daddy," he said.

He smiled and stood up. I was glad he felt so much better.

Suddenly he pointed and said, "Look, Daddy!" I looked.

It was a tree with low branches.

My daddy jumped up and down. "I can reach the branches. I want to climb it!" he said.

"Me, too!" I said.

But I was still my daddy, so I took a long look at the tree. It was awfully tall.

So I said, "All right, Son. You can climb this tree, and be careful not to climb too high."

But I was still pretending to be my daddy, and daddies don't mind worms.

So I said, "Son, worms aren't yucchy. They help flowers grow. If you get to know them, worms are very nice."

When Daddy saw me touch the worm, he said, "You sure are brave, Daddy."

He even touched the worm himself. I was proud of him.

Daddy ran ahead. I was a little worried. He wasn't looking where he was going.

"Look out, Son," I called to him. "Don't trip over that root!"

"What root?" he called back.

And just then he tripped.

My daddy cried. "Oh, Daddy," he said, "I hurt my finger!"

I looked at his finger. It had a little scratch.

"It'll be all right, Son," I said. "I'll make it stop hurting right now."

"You mean," he said, "I'll pretend to be you, and I'll do all the things you do when we walk in the woods?"

I said, "Yes, and I'll pretend to be *you,* and *I'll* do all the things *you* do."

"All right, *Daddy,"* said my daddy, and then he giggled and skipped off into the woods.

"Wait for me, *Son,"* I said as I ran after him.

Suddenly Daddy shouted, "Blecch!" I caught up with him, but I didn't see anything. Then I saw it. There was an ugly, crawly worm, right there on the ground.

"Look, Daddy!" said my daddy. "A worm! Worms are yucchy!"

"They sure are!" I said, and I didn't let the worm get too close to me.

by Daniel Wilcox

illustrated by
Mel Crawford

I'M MY
DADDY

"Let's pretend, Daddy," I said. "Let's pretend
that I'm the daddy and you're the son."
My daddy thought about it.

Library of Congress Cataloging in Publication Data
Wilcox, Daniel.
  I'm my mommy; I'm my daddy.
  "A Sesame Street book."
  Spine title; each story has special t.p.
  SUMMARY: Two stories explore the trials, tribu-
lations, and fun of being a parent from the point of
view of a mother and father.
  [1. Parent and child—Fiction] I. Wilcox, Dan-
iel. I'm my daddy. 1975. II. Crawford, Mel.
III. Title. IV. Title: I'm my daddy.

PZ7.W6455Im   [E]   75-5654

GOLDEN, A GOLDEN BOOK®, and GOLDEN PRESS® are
trademarks of Western Publishing Company, Inc. No part of
this book may be reproduced or copied in any form without
written permission from the publisher.

0-307-10499-0

Eighth Printing, 1978

My daddy took me for a walk in the woods.
We saw birds and trees—and even a deer.
I was thinking, and I thought up a good game.

I'm My Daddy